This book is a work of fiction. Char. business, places, organizations events and any incidents either are the product of the imagination or are used fictitiously. Any relationship or resemblance to actual persons living or dead, events or locales is entirely coincidental. The Mind of Melvin Copyright @ 2017 by Irvin Johnson. Printed in the United States of America.

No part of this book to be reproduced without written consent of the author except in the case of brief quotations embodied in articles or reviews. For information or movie rights contact the author at 7810 Rainer rd. se Olympia WA. 98513 Att. Melvin.

Best regards Irv

Forward

It was the fall of 1979

Mel loses his Father

His mother moves on so Mel has to move out.

Mel a child with borderline learning disabilities Struggle to make it on his own but what folks don't know is Mel is gifted with telekinesis.

Depression and desperation with some help from his new gift help him to become someone to recon with!

THE MIND OF MELVIN

Melvin

He had no friends although he knew he was a good person. Just a shy guy but somewhat goofy all the same. He came from a poor family that had little use for family values. On holidays and special occasions instead of gathering together they would all have other concerns about what each one was involved in. No one cared that the other didn't meet with them because they just expected their counter parts were on a mission to better their selves.

One such child of the Mc'Leo family was Melvin he was a middle child that came with its own problems such as to young for some things and too old for others. Melvin like to be called just Mel. That was a simple form of Melvin and it fit as Mel was a simple man. Mel never went to college and did only fair in high school, in fact the highest grade he ever brung home was a "D" Never the less it was passing and that was good enough in a family that was moving in five directions at once. Mel never exceled at any one thing unlike all the other kids.

> When school was over he tried some jobs but nothing paid much and the work at the bottom was hard in comparison to the rest of the world.

Oh, he learn how to get to work on time and how to give them a full day because that always seemed enough for Mel. Probably the worst thing was that he was still at home with Mom and dad.

The years went by and they teased him about leaving but he never thought in those terms and why should he. Mel had a place to sleep or eat and that was enough. Then one day it happened. A work accident left his father dead and with no one working that made anywhere near the Mortgage amount the house was put up for sale and his mother was to move in with his older sister. "Mel, you have to get your own place, you do understand don't you, after all you are twenty eight." "Um, okay I guess but where do I look?" "Oh just like your brothers and sisters did, in the newspaper under rentals."

Wow what a blow to a perfect life. Mel never figured having to leave not now, not ever no he hoped he was there forever. Ah but time and God decide all our fates and to him this was as devastating as could be.

"Here's the paper Mel, I circled some places I suggest you call." "But, mom I could go with you couldn't I?" "Not this time Melvin, not this time you have to leave the nest. I should have pushed you out sooner." "Anyway you're going to love being on your own, you will see." "Yeah, I guess so."

Mel called the numbers his mother had circled and then like it was unexpected a landlord was interested in renting to Mel.

"So kid you got any rental history?" "No, I have been living with mom and dad." "First place of your own them?" "Yes." "Okay no sense drilling you, I had a kid of my own that was a little slow leaving and I understand." "Thanks I guess." "You don't sound real happy about it." "Well my dad just died and I'm just not thinking to good." "Sorry to hear that, now bring eight hundred dollars on the first and were going to need the same for a damage deposit, you got any money?" "Ya, some." "Can you swing it, sixteen hundred dollars?" "Yes." "Good bring the clams and move on in."

"All right what's the address?" "Got a pen?" "Here we go,

"656 sap road N.W." "You get that?" "Yup, I'll come over tomorrow at noon." "See you then kid." "It's Melvin sir but my friends call me Mel." "Alright, see you Mel."

"Hey mom, I got a place moving in tomorrow." "That's nice Mel." "It's out of town a little on the old sap road." "That's nice dear." "Is it ok if I drive dad's truck to move?" "Yes, in fact I'm going to give it to you. I think he would have wanted you to have it." "I don't see why I have a bicycle." "You don't want to drive to Wally's restaurant day after day on that bike do you?" "I have been, but this is a lot further." "Good then its settled." "Mel, it could be rainy sometimes or cold and it's just better." "I may have to get a driver's license." "You never got one?" "Well, no I didn't have a need I guess." "But Melvin didn't you ever want to leave this town and maybe just see what else is out there?" "Nope, never did mom." "I'm going to drive you down to take your test, now you study this drivers test guide from your older sister." "Aw it's all changed by now." "Not that much besides in this town the test isn't that hard I've been told." "But, mom I am not going to need it." "To bad you're taking it and that's that." "Swell."

Time has a way of speeding up and as it did Mel got his licenses and on the first Mel moved in." "After unloading all his stuff he was running late for work and decided it wouldn't hurt to maybe drive. The old pickup truck run like a watch but somehow he never even imagine himself driving his father's truck.

"Say, Mel that's a pretty nice ride you're driving, how did you ever get something that good, rob a bank?" "It was my dad's, I think it's a Chevy." "How come you never drove it before?" "No driver license."

"Really, I couldn't wait to drive but you were able to get yours years ago, how come you didn't." "Don't know." "Maybe you're old man will sell it to you?" "He's dead, so it's mine." "Boy it's nice." "Thanks Bert."

Mel worked bussing table and dish washing for Wally, a heavy set man with a good work ethic and a bad disposition. He seldom talked to his employee's unless something was wrong. In fact if everything was running smooth Mel loved working there. However on more than one such occasion he would fire anyone who crossed his path, everyone that worked there knew this and on bad days stayed under the radar till things got better. Actually lots of small business works that way in a small town and if you're going to work there you better get used to it.

"Mel, where did you get a truck?" "From my dad, Wally he died and left it for me." "Sure you get all the breaks and I work my ass off here and your family don't even stop in and buy a damn hamburger, go figure!" "I could tell them Wally." "Yeah, you do that." "He leave you a bunch of money too?" "I don't know Wally." "Why not?" "I never asked I guess." "Oh brother you're a case, you better get to work." "Yep." Mel left work and when he got the time he thought maybe he would go back home and get his bicycle.

"Mom I'm home, anybody here?" "Melvin, I've fallen down and I can't get up, please help me." "Gee, mom I don't know what to do." "I know Mel you're a good boy get the phone over here for Mommy." "Yes, mom I will." "Mel dial that emergency number for me eeee plllse!" "Mom your talking funny mom are you okay, mom, mom talk to me mommy, sniff, sniff."

The lord gives and he takes away and so it was with Melvin mother. Mel wasn't sure what to do so he did the last thing his mom said and called the number and told the sheriff what happened and they were there in short order. Meanwhile Melvin held his moms head in his arms and weep, he loved her with every part of his body and soul and the fact that she died was almost more than he could deal with.

"Melvin, your moms better off now she went to haven you know. I am so very sorry for you and your family, can you get a hold of your sisters?" "Sniff, I guess so is she really gone?" "Yes, Melvin I know it hurts but you have to grow up real quick and try and sort all this stuff out, okay?" "I guess so sniff, I got to get my bicycle and take it to my house." "Yeah, you do that then call your sister's will you?" "Yes."

The coroner show up and Mel loaded his bike into the truck and as it drove away, Mel pulled over then vomited, he was sick. Lately everyone was dying or leaving for some reason and all his support mechanisms were gone. Mel had never felt so numb and hopeless in his whole life. He drove to his new home but to him it was a drug induced dream of gigantic proportions.

Mel walked up the stairs and into his new home. It wasn't fancy just an older house that was very clean. Boxes and garbage bags littered the floor as he never unpack or hung anything up yet, and now he didn't care. Mel had issues that were far reaching and made him a challenge to those around him and to himself.

"Well, I better get started and put all this stuff away." Mell, muttered. The house was furnished and he not thinking and very methodically sorted it out and put it away. Then being he was very tired, both mentally and physically, he lay down on the old couch and slept as if he were in a comma he never moved just lay there he wanted to cry but couldn't.

"Hi Mel, Mel is it?" "Yes." "Okay, I'll tell you just like I told that last guy." "No parties, I live in the next house over and I will hear you!" "Okay." "No fireworks or pets ever." "You got any pets?" "No." "I think we're going to get along just fine." "Yeah, um alright." "Here, sign this two year lease." "Two years I don't know." "How long were you at the last place?" "All my life I guess." "So see this is hardly nothing and if you want, two years from now maybe I'll let you renew it." "Sign right there by those X marks." "Atta boy, see you around, not too many girls ok?" "Haw ha just kidding see you later alligator." "Okay."

Mel was truly on his own and he still feeling low over everything. Melvin set for two hours in a chair and stared, sorta like always only this time he was trying to take a short mental vacation, sorta clear his mind. Mel stared at a pin wheel left by the last child and sticking out of a flower pot also left by the last occupants. The deeper he starred the more relaxed he became and as he stared he thought to himself if only he could have some control over his life. He starred still deeper and all of his other thoughts left him and then there was only him and the pin wheel. Mel thought to himself if only he could move the wheel at least there would be some little thing he could control in his miserable life, just even a small amount of movement, aw what a joke he should stop staring but then maybe it was the wind or maybe his imagination, who's to say, the pin wheel moved. It turned down on the right side, did he do it with his thoughts? Probably not but what if.

"Knock, knock." "Hello anybody there?" "Yes, I'm home." "Good here's some extra fuses you're going to need them if you overload any of the circuits in this old house, say you might want to buy some more blankets this place aint insulated worth shit, old homes were that way ya know." "Um okay." "See you in the funny papers kid." "Good bye."

Mel wanting to escape what was happing to him. To Mel any annoyance was a bad thing all he really wanted was to be alone, yes alone with his own thoughts. To Mel this was a safe haven far away from all the rules and troubles, it was the perfect place to live, in his mind. The smallest of noises bothered him greatly as they would not let Mel take his mental vacation.

It had been a very long and very difficult day. For Mel he was going to go to bed and live till morning in the sanctuary of his own mind. "He done all his usual things brushed his teeth, went pee then said his prayers. Sleep should come soon tonight after all it had been a somewhat difficult day, but no. He lay their real still not knowing what to expect in his new home. His mind pondered about ware wolves and Boogie men and all the other things that small simple children think of. Then he heard it, the sound of a million rats all-gnawing at the same time. Rats as big as cats with only one thing on their minds, Kill Mell! Kill Mel!

He hid under the covers and shook because he was as scared as he had ever been. If he only could reach that sleep area of his mind he might escape, he prayed for forgiveness of his every sin and awaited some miracle to rescue him, it never came and he sprung up then and turn on the lights. The gnawing subsided. Mel slept with the lights on tonight.

Mel got ready for work and made a peanut butter and jelly sandwich and cover his bread well to keep the rats from chewing on them in Mel's absence. He shaved and combed his hair but felt crummy because of all the sleep he lost.

"Hello, there buddy going to work today, eh" "Yes." "Sleep good last night?" "Well no, I kept hearing rats chewing on things it was scary sir." "You got a rat in there?" "Yes." "Did you read your lease any?" "Some." "Well if you did section three clearly states NO PETS!" "Now I suggest you set some traps or risk eviction, Haw ha." "Pretty funny don't ya think?" "Oh, yeah I guess, maybe." "Well, see ya soon ya big baboon, haw ha."

Mel took his lunch and headed for work. He hoped he wouldn't be late he really didn't know much about time management or how when traffic in the morning was heavier for a while then clear up for a couple of hours when you could make good time. Riding a bike he never had to think about Jams only about maybe what to ware so he could stay dry. Well it happened on this day that Mel found out the hard way about traffic jams. Mel sit in his pickup truck for what seemed hours and he was worried about maybe losing his job and that was all he had left. The car ahead of him just wouldn't move much. Just a little at a time. He went to his safe place in his mind and he thought how maybe he could push the car in front of him with his bare hands. Mel concentrated very hard when all of a sudden the tail light lenses that he in his mind was pushing broke in to a hundred pieces. Mel wondered if he was responsible but the traffic was moving now and so what, he had to get to work.

"Good morning Wally." "You look like hell and your ten minutes late you little squid, now get you sorry ass to work." "Alright I will." "Hey, Mel I heard Wally chewed your ass out are you going to quite?" "No." "Well if you are my brothers looking for a job and this one is close." "No, not yet I guess, should I?" "Boy, you are simple." "Cut that talking crap off back there and just do your job Melvin!" "Okay."

Mel thought all day how he could get even with Wally but not lose his job, he would have to be careful. Funny how your mind wonders while doing mindless task like washing dishes and sorting knives, forks and spoons. Mel had done this a hundred thousand times. Mel stared at the wall and focus himself on one small spot, this is where he put his hate and small but evil ideas. Today was not much different except what had occurred earlier with the taillight on the way in and it made him concentrate all the harder. He could see big fat Wally and those bright red suspenders growling insults and bossing everyone around as usual, not this day he focus in his mind on breaking Wally's suspender, on both sides.

Melvin, we need some more plates out here you moron." "Would you hurry up, sheeze I should have hired a monkey." With one last push from his mind Mel went for more plates.

 "Har, har, har, har, Wally's pants are down around his ankles'!"

Wally fell with a full plate of spaghetti and meatballs that were smashed and spaghetti was on his white tee shirt and he was very orange and extremely mad.

"Dam lousy no good suspenders what the hell you looking at lady, help me up you idiots, for crying out loud." "Get Mell out here and clean this, God damn dump up!"

"Where should I put the plates Mel?" "You nincompoop put them up your ass, for all I care." "But you said you wanted them." "Over there you stodge!" "Now mop this crap up, how the hell shit like this keep happens I'll never know." "Nancy, you run the place I'm going to go home and get a good pair of these rotten suspenders!" "Yes, Wally sorry you fell I hope you weren't hurt too bad." "Oh, I'll be fine now get something done will you!" "Mel wasn't that the craziest thing you ever seen?" "Um, he sorta had it coming." "Boy you said a mouthful and a lot worse, what a dam tyrant." "So Mel, how's your new home going?" "I got rats." "You do why don't you get a cat?" "I am afraid of cats, they don't like me." "Yeah, were all a little goofy around here I guess."

Mel went back to picking up dishes and help clean up the mess from Wally falling. Later back at the dish rack he sat down and took a break as was customary. He ate his lunch in the back out of site and out of mind. Mel was picking his rather large nose when Nancy came back to check on him and caught him.

"Mel are you picking your nose?" "Yep." "

Sheeze, let us know when you find it." "Um okay." "I've got to get the hell out of this place, weirdest job I've ever had." "Why do you say that, Nancy?" "You really don't get it, do you?" "Get what?" "This place is a crappy place to work." "I am just here because this was all I could find but there's better places to work, in fact much better." "So?" "You're hopeless!"

Mel wondered what she meant aren't all jobs this terrible? He had been going here for over twelve years and it never occurred to him that there might be something better. Mel remembers once that Wally wanted to get him into being a waiter and be able to get tips and basically make more take home pay, but Mel declined and wondered why a guy couldn't just be good at what he did? Simple job, simple guy.

"Mel, get off your lazy ass and get back to those dishes, will you?" "All Right." Nancy, did things go okay when I was gone? "Yes Wally just peachy." "I'll bet!"

Mel worked with a certain amount of Vigor the rest of the day. He wasn't sure he done all these things but if he did, well that would be just swell. At the end of the shift Wally gave Mell a bunch of trash to drop off at the dump because it was on his way home. Mell didn't mind as he could hardly tell when he was being taken advantage of.

"Boy you're a weird renter, you're sure coming in here late did you do anything about those little mice?" "No, not yet, I just sleep with the lights on." "Oh, brother that's just idiotic, you aren't on drugs or something are you?" "I wouldn't put up with that, nope out you'll go."

"No, I don't do that, just say no." "Well alright." "I'm just warning you." "You going to get a cat, I got one you know I could bring him over tomorrow, whatcha think?" "No, I'm okay." "All right sleep tight don't let the bed bugs bite har, har." "Good night."

Mel, hit the hay and left the lights on but this time only in the bedroom so the landlord wouldn't get mad. When he listen closely he could still hear them gnawing in the walls, and it terrified him. He stayed in bed and hid under the covers where he prayed half the night and then as if his prayers were maybe answered he fell asleep because of exhaustion.

Early in the morning and time to make his lunch, something he was not used to doing because in the past his mother always made it for him. Peanut butter and jelly was a great meal in fact if he had to he could survive on it.

He had nothing else like his mom used to add but thought if he was still hungry he could eat some leftover food from a customers. Maybe a roll, maybe some toast or possible a waffle that was untouched and that was only breakfast. Mel was learning about traffic and this time left thirty minutes early. The backup was light today and Mel had no trouble.

"Good morning Wally." "Oh, looks like the Moron decide to get here on time take a look everybody, haw ha." "Not much to say do ya Melvin?" "No sir." "Haw ha."

The day began swift as the breakfast crowd was heavy this morning and Mel was having a hard time keeping up with enough clean plates for all the customers.

"Mell don't let me down, you better get your sorry ass in gear, were busier than a one armed paper hanger out here now step on it will ya?" "Okay."

If only there was some way he could slow things down. Everyday lately just got worse and Wally was too cheap to hire any extra help. And why should he with a guy like Mel he could kick around. Then Mel thought real hard about what if the grill run out of gas or just stopped getting hot. He would have to try while he worked hard. Behold, Mel stopped the grill and the complaints were coming in about cold food.

"What the hell going on around here, you cooks are putting out cold food!" "You dummies ever think about turn the dam thing up." We can't Wally I think it quit." "That's impossible did you imbeciles turn off the main valve to get out of work, so help me if you did." "We never touched anything Wally it just quit!" "Let me in

26

there for crying out loud, I'll fix the piece of crap!" "Yeah go ahead." "Did you just call me a GOAT HEAD?" "NO, NO we just said go ahead." "Hmmm, I'll bet you did."

Well things went from bad to worse and finally Wally, called the gas company and give them a piece of his mind. He was as foul as I ever heard him with insults to the company's mother and beyond her grave.

 Back over at the other end of the line was a man who had a theory about the more you bitched the longer he would take to repair.

"Ya, I hear you Wally but can't get over there till oh, oh Tuesday, yep, Tuesday I guess about five." "Well see that you do!"

Then Wally slammed down the phone and said. "You people got to go till Wednesday. I can't pay you birds to just stand around doing nothing, now clear out of here will ya!" "Good night Wally." "What's good about it?" "Sorry, Wally about the gas."

"Mel you get the hell out of here or so help me I'll throw you out!" "Um, okay I guess."

The road home at this hour was very good with very little traffic, so Mel stopped to get some snacks and some traps for mice.

"You got some rats?" "Just mice I think." "Well out here in the country you better get used to the little varmints ha, haw." "Yeah." "That all you eating nowadays ding dongs and Twinkies?" "I got peanut butter and jelly." "Good for you, like I care." "Good bye." "Bye, bye." "Boy we sure get em in here."

Mell drove home and as sure as the sun shines there was his good old landlord there to greet him.

"Say, Melvin I gotcha that cat just like I promised and I heard he's one hell of a mouser." "Um, no thanks I got some mice traps." "Those things only catches the little ones but this cat will get them as big as him almost, and he won't back down even if they bite him and tear the flesh right off him." "Now if I were you I'd take the cat, and what the hell he's free. He will work all night for just a little food, so whatcha say?" "Oh, alright I guess, does he have a name?" "Oh, eh, um, Killer that's it Killer the cat." "You go ahead and get in there and I'll put him in there with you and you don't open that door or he may make a run for it." "Okay, I think but okay." "So Melvin you ever been around a cat before or you ever had one of your own?" "No." "Ha, it's very easy you just smear some butter on his feet and when he licks it off he thinks he's at home." "Yeah." "Yup he will be loyal to you all his life, even to his dying day but don't ever make him mad, no sir he will scratch your eyes out!" "Really?" "Just be nice to old killer and you two will get along just fine." "I am not so sure." "You're going to be a natural now get in there and I'll send him in. Oh, he might be a bit hard to catch at first but don't worry he will settle down as soon as you put that butter on his paws." "Peanut butter okay?" "Even better well got to go." "Thanks, I guess." "Here kitty, kitty here Killer, nice Kitty" "Wow that wasn't nice, you hurt me, you bad kitty, now hold still while I put some peanut butter on your feet." "I'll just flip you over, **hey you're a, bad cat that hurt me!" "You make in me bleed, you hurt Mel!"**

"**B**ad kitty cat." "No food for you tonight."

Mel went over and sat on the couch and glared at the cat. The cat was still very upset and humped his back then hissed in the corner. Mel wanted to be friends with the cat on several levels, in fact he needed to. Well making friends with a wild cat is no fun and requires a certain amount of patience. Mel glared deep into the cat's eyes and thought if only there was some way to tell the cat that he wasn't going to hurt him.

Then he had a thought that maybe what was wrong was the cat seen him as a big monster and if Mel were to get down and look deep into its eyes on its own level maybe he could get through to him.

"Here kitty, kitty," Mel stared hard into the cats eyes and thought if only he could just make him wink, and wink back at Mel then maybe it would understand Mel. Mel stared and got up to one foot slowly and then he done as Mel always done and that is go into his own world for just a second. Mel winked at the cat and just like he had imagined the cat winked back! Mel moved in closer," **Eyowww that smarts you bad cat I hate you!**" Killer clawed Mel's nose very badly. The cat backed into a corner and hissed then growled like never before. Mel left the cat there and hurried off to bed and shut his door so the cat could not get him in his sleep.

Mel wasn't sleeping so good, worrying about what if he had to use the bathroom in the night would that cat attack him? The rats were still doing their gnawing and getting to sleep was a challenge to say the least. What if they came through the walls in the bedroom where the cat was not there, who would help him, maybe they would bite his nose or worse crawl in bed with Mel, he pulled the covers tighter then over his head and cried for he knew one false move and he was a goner. But even fear has its limits and after a while Mel did fall to sleep. Sometime in the night the cat got cold and having no bedding Killer went in search of a place to sleep. Cats are very curious by nature and he was able to push the bedroom door open and jumped up on Mel's bed and sleep at his feet. Mel slept well and deep listening to killers soft purring.

"Noooooo, you cat, go, go, bad cat!" Killer ran being very startled as he was just entering his deep sleep. Meanwhile Mel made a mad dash to the bathroom and did as much as he could to be ready for work and to not have to travel near that wild animal! Then came the time to leave and he knew he would have to be braver than he had ever been before, he opened the door slowly and looked around. Killer was in the window seal by the front door, Mel took all his courage and moved real slowly then opened the front door and left it that way, wide open, then he returned to the kitchen and started banging the cupboard doors back and forth making noise to scare the cat out. "Go on you, get out you hurt me you bad cat, I hate you." Mel glared some more at the cat from afar and then he winked. It worked the cat was down and out of there like a rocket ship to Mars. "Whew, that was close." Mel sat on a stool with a small mouse on the counter eating off the dirty knife he had left when he tried to spread peanut butter on Killers feet.

Mel turned his head and saw it.

"Awwww, go away I hate you too!" Mel holler was very

effective and the small mouse left in a hurry. Mel wouldn't be bringing a lunch today it just wasn't safe in his home, so he left for work."

"Good morning Wally." "WHATEVER!" "Hey Melvin, your Sister called said you should call here back, oh yeah on your own damn time!" "Um, okay I guess." "You guess, you imbecile it's you Sister for crying out loud and I told her you would, so you will, comprehend-a?" "Yes I will."

Mel worked until he got a break and then proceeded to call his Sister with the number Wally had gave him.

"Hello, Sissy you wanted me to call?" "Yes of Corse Melvin, how are you doing?" "Oh alright I guess I'm moved in now like mom wanted." "That's nice Mel do you have a good landlord?" "Sorta too good he's always around, checking on me." "Oh, Mel he probably just lonely." "Yup." "How's your job going huh?" "Alright, I guess sure a long drive." "You just get up earlier that's all there is to it Melvin, okay?" "Okay Sis." "Well say good bye Mel and I love you." "I love you too Sis."

Back on the job Mel thought to himself he sure was hungry but he would have to wait till Wally went somewhere or lunch time. He gather up some dishes in the dining room to take back and clean up for the next meals when he noticed that one had a steak on the plate that someone never took a bite out of. It was cold and he was supposed to throw it out but when he had a chance in between his other duty's he ate it.

"Say Mel didn't you bring your lunch today?" "Oh, I left in a hurry and forgot." "Here pal you can have half of mine." "Gee thanks, does this mean were friends?" "Eh, sure, were friends." "Thanks, Nancy you're nice." "Oh, you would do it for me wouldn't you?" "Yes." "Nancy do you like Wally?" "Oh God no, I hate that guy but he's the boss you know." "Yeah." "Nancy do you have rats at your home?" "No, why would I?" "Nothing, just wondered."

Mel travel home as soon as he could not wanting to enter his house after dark because of the cat and the rats. Then naturally he had to dump some more trash for Wally. He hurried home it was still light out and once again there was his old friend the Landlord.

"Good evening Melvin, make any headway with those little shrews?" "You mean the rats?" "Er, mice?" "No, the cat ran away and the mice were eating my peanut butter." "I can get you another if you like?" "Cat?" "Yep, I'll bring him tomorrow if you want." "No, that's okay I bought some traps I'll try them I think." "Suit yourself, ya know that's really not a big deal out here in the country half of all the houses have mice." "Is that so?" "Fact." "I got to go I got stuff to do." "You need any help I am just over there in that house." "You just call okay?" "Okay."

Mel entered the house again and looked for mice on the counter. He found some evidence that they had indeed been up there eating the last of the old peanut butter knife. Mel cleaned the counter and the knife then made his lunch and put it in the refrigerator where he figured it would be safe. Then he went about setting traps and hoping he could get the little rascals. He brushed his teeth and jumped into bed, and prayed tonight might be better. Well it was not as noisy as before. And as the night unfolded it got noisier, except most of the noise was from the kitchen and Mel was afraid to witness their deaths, and so he heard them flopping and squealing all night, and then there was silence. Mel quickly went to sleep.

Driving down the highway Mel waved at the Landlord and moved quickly out of his sight as he was starting to dislike his too friendly of visits.

 Today he thought he had won something when he put the mouse's that were killed by his hand and left to suffer unmercifully in the trash. He smiled when he thought what a blessing it was to be able to live without worrying all night long about some critter biting his fingers. The radio was playing we are the champions and Mel knew they were singing his song, he felt more confident than he had in a long, long time. He whipped into the parking lot of Wally's Restaurant Café.

"God morning Nancy, you look nice today." "Um, I am sorta busy setting up right now so don't have time to chit chat just this moment Mel." "Alright." "Good morning Wally." "You knucklehead, every sense you got that free truck your weirder." "I am not." "See, there you go acting like I ought to fire you!"

Mel said not a word but went to his work station and started to work.

"What did that last remark short out your brain you idiot?" "No." "Good, now how about putting in a full day's damn work for a change you twit!" "Um, okay."

Mel figured maybe Wally was upset because he was late that one day and didn't put in a full day like Wally expected.

"Why do you let him bully you like that Mel?" "Oh, it's okay I'm used to it and I like it here sorta." "You are hopeless Mel." "I Know." "Well one of these days I am getting so far away from this place and all Wally's insults it's not even funny, maybe Montana or Idaho." "Can I go too, I'm special, that's what my mom say's?" "No, lamb chop, this may be okay for you, beings that maybe you are special." "You should stay and keep Wally inline." "Um okay."

Mel thought about what Nancy had said and it had an effect on him as he could be the only one that could keep Wally in line. He would do like she said, maybe make this a better place.

"Nancy, Nancy, why the hell is this cash count coming up short are you trying to rip me off?" "No Wally, look under the drawer there's a hundred dollar bill in there." "Ya, well it better be or you're going down that highway, you hear me lady!" "I hear you Wally." "Yeah and cut the attitude will you." "Okay."

Nancy went to the rest room where she could get away from Wally and she cried for a full two minutes, Mel walking by and heard her crying and it made him sad. He would have to do something, he didn't exactly know what but something to make Wally's day much harder.

Mel washed the dishes and dried and stacked those in the kitchen there were many and after a while in the repetition of it he stared at his spot in the wall and thought about getting Wally.

He knew Wally's ever habit and move for about every day for a long time. Besides he knew that in ten minutes Wally would hog the men's bathroom for about one hour straight. The knob on the door was loose anyway, so what if it broke completely would any one try to get him help right away, he doubted it.

"Hey!" "Somebody get me out of here!" "Damit, I mean it get me out or I'll fire the whole bunch of you!" "What's the problem Wally, haw ha?" "Nancy is that your voice you get me out of here will you?" "Gee, Wally I don't know what to do, ha haw." "Oh very funny is it, now that I'm stuck in here get this door open will you?" "What's wrong Wally?" "How the hell should I know the latch is broken?" "Do you want a butter knife I could slip one under the door?" "Yeah I guess." "What's taking so long?" Nancy!" NANCY!" "Okay, I had to wait on a customer. "Piss on them, get me the hell out of here, you hear me you nitwit." "Wally, I'm trying to help you but if you call me names, I am not!" "Well, get that moron in the back to help me!" "Mel?" "Yes, for crying out loud how many MORONS you think we got?" "That's not nice to say about Mel, Wally." "Like I give a rat's ass about his poor little feelings now get that goofy kid and get me out!" "Mel is special, not goofy Wally, I'll go get him." "Yeah you better you just better or I'll." "You'll what Wally?" "Oh, nothing now get him will you?" "That's better." "Big deal oh gee, I got manners so what do I look like I'm Miss Manners?" "Hey, Wally did you get stuck in there?" "No, I'm taking a vacation in the Alps, you nincompoop!" "Can I help you Wally you look like you're locked in?" "No shit Sherlock now go get some tools were going to have to take this lock apart." "Ok, can I eat my lunch first Wally?" "You do and I'll put your hands in the deep fryer you understand don't you Melvin?" "Ouch, yes I'll wait I guess." "Hurry will you I got to get to the bank today and sign a loan, it's real damn important you idiot!" "Wally!" "Okay I'll be nice, but hurry him up will you?" "Okay were going to go look for some tools."

 Mel look but ate his sandwich while he looked, Nancy help him while she ate a piece of cherry pie.

"Were back Wally." "Were back Wally, the two of you don't add up to one half, where the hell have you been I was going to send some flowers I thought you were dead?" "We went as fast as we could Wally." "Somehow I believe that." "You two take the screws out of the door lock, will you?" "We got the wrong type of screw driver." "Ya, you would!" "I'll go get another Wally." "You do that you dumb shit!" "What did you say?" "Nothing get that screwdriver!" "I came back Wally did you need something else?" "Yeah a shotgun to shoot you, now go get the right screwdriver, Nancy help him." "What?" "Get the rotten screw driver!" "Okay." "Oh brother!" "Why lord, I'm employing a bunch of dim-wits." "Wally, I got all the tools and I'm taking the little screws out for you." "Oh, that's nice you ninny!" "Only two left Wally, boy them things are in there." "Keep working you, you, Melvin." "Okay Wally, I am." "Would you hurry?" "Okay Wally only one more left." "Uh oh." "What's wrong fathead." "Gee, Wally the screwdriver is broken and the tip is rounded off I think." "Go out in the back of my car in the trunk I have some more in there, now hurry!" "Okay." "Hey, can you hear me, hey you're going to need the keys, and there in my pocket!" "Mel, where did that dummy go anyway?" "Is

Anybody listening to me?" "HEY!" "Sheeze." "Wally I'm back, and guess what?" "Here's the keys you moron." "Um, thanks Wally I'll be right back." "I ought to trade you for a dog and shoot the damn dog, you imbecile." "Nancy, have you seen that kid?" "Wally relax, he's out in your car in the trunk." "Well tell him to hurry, will you?" "Um, Melvin Wally said to hurry." "Okay, I will." "He said he's hurrying." "Well tell him to hurry faster will you?" "Sure, Wally I got some customers so don't worry he will be here any time now." "He must be doing the Tennessee bird walk." "Here I come Wally I got the right one." "Swell, just swell." "Almost got it Wally, there you go now just pull on the latch okay?" "Thank god I'm out of there I was ready to go insane in there." "Block this door off and I'll go get a new lock." "But what about my lunch, Wally?" "You better block it first or I'll have your head on a stick you pathetic turd." "Alright, I will Wally, sure glade you're out."

Mel and Nancy shared a hamburger on the house while Wally the Hun went looking for a lock. Wally got back just about closing time and started repairing the door. Wally forgot to send the trash with Mel as usual. This made Mel happy today then Mel thought the broken lock please him too. The drive home today was almost effort less and he arrived early.

"There's my boy, how you doing Mel?" "Good I guess made it home early today." "Well that s good." "Say did you ever get rid of them pest?" "I think so sir." "Great it was the cat huh?" "No, I caught them in some traps." "Did you now, well how is old Killer anyway?" "I don't know he ran away." "Yep, I know I caught em for you and I put him back in your house for you." "But I had it locked." "Well, every good Land Lord has a pass key, haw ha." "Gee that seems sorta bad." "Naww, that's not bad what if you were on fire and I saved you and killer from getting burnt up?" "Okay I guess." "Sure it is that's why we got one." "Alright." "That cat seems wild." "Nope he's a charmer you two just got to get used to each other's." "Well see you later I'm going inside now." "I know when I'm getting the bums rush I can take a hint." "Good night." "Yes, good night."

Mel slammed the door and was starting to get annoyed with the land lord letting himself in plus bringing back that cat, Killer. Mel looked around to see that nothing was missing or messed with and then he seen the cat. It was on the foot of Mel's bed. Mel looked to see if the land lord was still there and then opened the door to outside and then opened the bedroom door and he went for a shower thinking the cat would most likely leave on its own. When he was ready for bed he looked in the bedroom and Killer was still there. Mel had been through a lot today and thought he could deal with the cat tomorrow then crawled into bed. The cat stayed at his feet and purred all night till late then moved closer to Mel's head as he wanted to be closer to his new master. When Mel awoke he was startled but when he heard killer purring softly he reach up from the covers and gently stroked his new pet.

Back at work Nancy and Mel and a few other waitresses were very cheery today. It seems they delighted in Wally's misery. They laughed throughout the day while thinking about how helpless he was. "Good morning Wally." "What's good about it?" "I don't know." "You wouldn't you Democrat." "Good morning Wally, how are you?" "I am just great like you guys care." "We do Wally." "Humph!" "And how are you doing Mel?" "Me, oh okay I guess Nancy, want to eat lunch together?" "Yes it's a date!"

Mel was beside himself he had never had a date in his whole life, but now there he was going to lunch with the prettiest girl he had ever seen. He worked hard and really didn't have any real problems or worries. In Mel's life this was one of the best days ever. It was even better than a sixteenth birthday party his mom had given him.

"Gee Mel you're at lunch early, did you get all your stuff done early?" "Yes Nancy, so I could go on our date." "Do you want one of my peanut butter sandwiches?" "Eh, that's okay Mel but I got my own thanks any way, you're a good boy." "Um, I think you pretty." "I'll bet you do, sweet Mel, I'll bet you do." "I got, Twinkie you want half?" "That okay, I'm good Mel." "Oh alright I thought you like me." "I do Mel." "Wally was sure funny yesterday." "Boy, you can say that again." Wally was sure funny yesterday." "Well I'm about done now I got to get back to work." "But you never ate your pickle." "Would you like it Mel?" "Yes." "It's all yours Mel, it's all yours." "Thank you Nancy."

After downing a pickle Mel went back to work. Wally came in to see Mel.

"Mel I found some damn food left on a fork this morning can you clean them better and stay away from Nancy will you?" "Um all right." "Good, you dirty silverware Casanova, you do that!" "That kid is dumber than a box of rocks."

Mel could take a few insults about himself personally because he realize he wasn't like everyone else, but the comment about Nancy, the girl that just gave him a dill pickle, well that's pushing things real far. He again stared at his spot and this time he glared harder, then a small white sphere formed. He wished Wally wasn't so mean and much weaker so he couldn't inforce his insults, or maybe just dumber. Well, all things have a season and Mel thought all things happened for a reason. He wasn't sure what was happening but it was as if all Mel's hatred toward Wally was finding it's self in that ball and then he watched it leave and enter Wally's head. Wally fell to the floor and the medics were called.

"Wow, that was awful Mel I think old Wally just had a stroke I hope he's ok." "You do?" "Well sure I wouldn't wish that on any one." "But, Wally was mean man." "Well Mel he probably had it coming but still things like that are just terrible don't you think?" "No." "Whatever, well we well just have to see how he is. If he gets out of the hospital, now wont we?" "Uh huh." "Will Wally's restaurant be open tomorrow?" "Oh yes, his wife Martha will run it, she is real nice, you will like her." "Oh boy I can't hardly wait."

Mel drove home again without the usual load of garbage Wally pilled on for him to dump on his own time. Mel tried whistling. He whipped his truck in the yard and felt just a little bit forceful for once in his life. What a day! First date the boss gets sick and a pickle plus no garbage, he entered his home and set on the couch petting his cat.

"Hi killer did you have a good day?" "I'll bet you did you cute kitty here look Melvin in the eye." "Owww, that hurt you moron how would you like to look cross-eyed all your life?"

Then Mel stared at the spot on the wall he had seen earlier and again he was able to make a bright but smaller sphere, and it went to killer and settled on his head, then it vanished.

"You sorta look good that way killer, I hope you understand, it was for your own good."

After that Mel was more tired than he could ever remember and he went to bed and slept like never before.

Mel woke up refreshed, zippier than ever. He said, "Good morning killer" then went for his shower and hurried off to work.

"Good morning Nancy, you sure look pretty today." "Aww, thanks Melvin." "Melvin, this is Martha, Wally's wife, today she is in charge so do anything she says okay?" "Um, yes." Melvin you just do what you were doing before." "Okay you can call me Mel." "I'll make a note of it." "Is Wally okay?" "The doctors are keeping him in till he's feeling better so he can come back to work." "Oh." "Nancy do you want to have lunch with me again?" "Ah, I got to go out today so maybe later in the week," "Alright."

Mel felt hurt but worked just the same, he knew she liked him but she was beginning to ignore him and that hurt him. The work went slow today and without a tormentor it seemed to drag on. Mel wondered in his thoughts if he was the one who made Wally's suspenders break, or the lock to break and even Wally's sudden stroke, maybe all of those things were nothing more than a string of coincidence and just Radom luck, yeah that's probably what it was but he did have a cross eyed cat, he sure didn't imagine that and he did see that taillight break right before his eyes then on the other hand maybe it was broken before and just picked that time to break so many questions and this time he found he had a lot more time to ponder these things.

"Well good night Nancy." "Good night to you too Mel, see you tomorrow." "Um, did I tell you about my cat, its cross eyed." "That's nice Mel." "You're lucky again you don't have to haul Wally's garbage again, but you know what?" "What." "It really needs to be hauled bad it's starting to pile up and stink, could you do it for me?" "Um, sure Nancy I will."

Mel loaded the garbage and hauled it off, he really didn't want to but to get a chance to do Nancy a favor well it sorta rounded out the day. He thought so much of her. Deep in his mind she reminded him of his Mother when she was younger. He could even see her as his lover, she was so nice plus always so thoughtful, yes even protective from Wally's raves and to Mel she was the embodiment of everything nice in the world.

He dumped the trash then watched a rat run out of the ruble and it stared at Melvin as if he knew what Mel had done to his brothers. Mel stared back and slowly the rat slipped away. Mel drove home and thought about the rat then pondered if he had made it leave?

"Good evening Mel, you running a little late?" "Oh yeah, I had to haul some trash to the dump." "How are you and that cat getting along now?" "You know other than it purrs all the time real well." "You know you can let him out now and he won't run off any more if he likes you." "Yes, I suppose I should it does make some smelly messes on the floor." "Look you ruin that house and I'll kick you out, now I don't want that house full of cat shit so you let old eh, killer out in the day time will you." "Yes." "I got to go to bed now." "I am tired." "Well good night." "Night."

Mel closed the door and went inside and cleaned up a whole lot of cat crap that killer had left. That landlord was starting to get on his Nevers seems he is always there when Mel got home and always checking on him. He was so nosy Mel didn't know why but he just didn't like him much.

 Being late Killer and Mel hit the sack. Mel looked at Killers eyes and wondered if maybe they weren't sorta like that from the start. He went to sleep and dreamed of Nancy.

Mel washed his hand and made his lunch while Killer tried to watch, it was not easy when his eyes were crossed, still he tried and he rubbed his back up against Mel's legs.

"Out you go Killer, be careful hunting in your condition."

Mel started the big Chevrolet Truck and drove to work just like every other day.

"Good morning Nancy, did I tell you about my cat his name is Killer." "That's creepy."

"I'm counting in this money Mel so don't talk to me right now." "Yes."

Mel worked till lunch and then went in search of Nancy so he could have lunch with her and tell her about his friend, killer. He passed Martha in the hallway. Martha caught up with Mel and complimented him on his performance today, which had been well.

"Mel, I think you're awesome." "Oh?"

"Nancy can I eat with you?" "Oh go ahead." "Did you hear what Martha said about you?" "Yes, she said I was a possum." No Mel, she said you were awesome that means terrific!" "Oh, well you called me a goat head." "What?" "Yes, when I asked if I could eat lunch with you, then you said, goat head." "No!" "I said, go ahead, and now sit down." "You're goofy, and that's why I think I like you." "I like you too." "Did I tell you about my cat?" "Oh, go um, do it." "His name is killer he's got crossed eyes." "Siamese?" "No just one."

"His name is killer." "Killer the cross eyed cat, that's a good one, haw ha." "Single man are you?" "Yes." "I couldn't have guessed in a hundred years." "Really?" "No." "Well lunch is over got to get back before we get busy." "Ugg, me too."

Mel was starting to like Nancy more and more. Nancy, well she felt that Mel was a needy person that could use some positive assurance from time to time. Nothing that could be taken wrong just positive reinforcement to build his confidents a bit. Unfortunately Mel looked at Nancy with eyes that wanted so much more. He had never had anybody and was scared but with Nancy he felt somewhat safe, yes, maybe he would ask her out. Mel figured the worst that could happen is that she would yell at him and after all of Wally's yelling he knew he could take it.

At home and in the house without that Landlord bugging him, he made his lunch for tomorrow and then stayed on the couch with Killer.

"Caught any mice lately?" "Purrrer, purr." "Yeah you're a lot like me you don't talk much do you?" "It's okay I'm the quite type too."

Mel and killer went to bed and now Killer slept with his head up on the pillow with Mel. Killer's tail curled around Mel's head and tickled him sometimes. Killer was not his best friend but he was a good friend and good friends are hard to find.

It was a shame about his eyes and Mel was pretty sure it interfered with his hunting.

Up a bit late today Mel would have to hurry again he hoped the traffic lights would work in his favor. The traffic was heavy and it wasn't long before he was stalled. He was more than a little upset at something he had little control over or did he? Five cars ahead he could see and stare at the traffic light then he concentrated on them to change and they did out of sequence and early. He travelled through. Mel looked in his rear view mirror and seen an awful wreck it was a good thing he got through when he did he thought. Mel arrived on time and punched the clock one full minute ahead of starting time.

"Good morning Mel." "Good morning Mrs. Mack." "Oh please, call me Martha, Melvin." "Yes, Martha." "Good morning Nancy." "Oh, good morning Wally." "You want to go out for dinner some time?" "With you?" "Yes, I will pay." "As inviting as that sounds I have to say no, my boyfriend wouldn't like it." "Okay."

Boy that was awkward he thought she would just say no, but it seemed that if she didn't have a boyfriend she would. Most guys would give up at this point but Melvin was no ordinary guy. He would have to get a look at this boyfriend. Maybe he would be just like him or big, ugly and smelly. Now he had to see him.

"Well Melvin, would you like to join me for lunch?" "Oh, boy Nancy I sure would." "Um, okay I guess let's sit here in the lunchroom." "I made an extra peanut butter sandwich just for you, here." "I'm not very hungry Mel, why don't you eat it." "Okay." "Mel, do you want my apple?" "Yes, thank you Nancy." "Nancy do you like Martha?" "Oh, God yes such an improvement over Wally." "Unfortunately I heard Wally will be back next week unless he has complications." "What's complications?" "Oh, you know trouble with his heart again." "Oh." "Well, Mel I hate him but I don't hope he gets worse I wouldn't wish that on anybody." "You wouldn't?" "Well no." "Time to go back." "Thanks for the apple." "Sure."

Back at work Mel was in his strange mood again and he pondered how someone as nice as Nancy could have a boyfriend.

Worse yet one that would keep her from going out with him. He would have to hang around and see what he looks like when he arrives at night to pick her up. It's hard to hate someone you never met, still he must try, perhaps he could give him a headache, he stared at his spot in the kitchen on the wall that he had starred at before his thoughts were pure and hateful and all aimed at a unknown boyfriend. Mel was in a trance and never realized that the sink was overflowing until he heard.

"What the hell do you think you're doing you really are a nitwit!" "Um, oh sorry." "Wake up you dummy or lose your job maybe Wally was right you are an imbecile!" "I didn't mean it I was thinking." "That's a laugh, you are the dumbest dishwasher we've ever had!" "Can you even read?" "Um, some." "Well, there's one bigger idiot here and that's Wally for hiring you, now clean this mess up and quite thinking so much, just do your job!" "Yes, Martha."

Mel worked on then at the end of the day he waited around to see Nancy's boyfriend. Then at last he showed up and it was a good thing because Mel was getting tired of peeking out of the bathroom door.

"Hey baby, sorry I'm late I had the damness   headache, I had to stop I was going cross eyed and couldn't drive but I feel good now give me a kiss." "Oh Max, I was so worried about you it's been a strange day not as bad as when Wally's here but strange all the same." "Let Max make it all better. I was working out at the gym and thinking about you real strong still want to marry me?" "Max, you know I do and the sooner the better." "Let's go baby, maybe I'll let you whisper in my ear har, har."

Max, Nancy's boyfriend was huge and all muscle he could tear Mel the weenie arm from limb to limb and not even break into a sweat.

Mel hated him very much and felt very threatened by his very existence. He also knew how hopeless it was plus he was very use to disappointment in his life. He would have to think some on what he could do next then. Mel started his Dads truck and drove home to his cross eyed cat Killer, his only true friend.

Mel tossed and turned he Knew he really loved Nancy because she was the only female besides his mom who took the least interest in him and she gave him a pickle and apple.

She must have feelings for him too. It is true when someone is in love with someone that in their mind they can do no wrong they see them in a better light even their very words come out musically and fulfilling and this was the case with Nancy the best and prettiest girl on the face of Melvin's earth. Somehow, someway even though it may take years, he would have to have her for his very own.

Rising early the weather had turned cold and a light rain fell on the truck windshield as he traveled to work. Yes, work where he could look at his girl, Nancy the woman of his desirers. Today he would do something to make her notice him.

"Good morning Nancy, I seen you're boyfriend last night." "Yes, Max picked me up, he's been working out and getting big muscles." "What is his Name?" "Max, he is a drywall worker." "I am so proud of him were going to get married!" "Um, oh." "I will see you at lunch I guess." "Okay."

Working back in the kitchen Mel thought about big ole, Max. What could he do to discourage him from coming over and marrying the girl of his dreams. Maybe if he broke his leg. Mel, could spend some quality time with Nancy then she might forget him. He had never broke anything of that magnitude before. In fact he was never really sure he done anything at all, he would just have to have faith that he could do such a thing. He decided to try it when he got home where it was quite and he could have no distractions.

All Mel's life he had been very single minded and couldn't do more than one thing at a time. He was aware that he was different than others. Well, it seems as nature has a way of becoming the great equalizer and so it was with Mel, what he lacked in brain power he made up with thought power and even though he had not had to use it much before he moved out on his own. He somewhat knew what was going on. He worked hard and waited for the time he could drive home.

The road was slick and as Mel left his tires spun for one hundred yards then Mel realized the need to let off and drive safe. He loved hot rodding the old pickup, it was a thrill he had never had before. By the time he got home the driveway was muddy and the truck made ruts six inches deep. Walking to the house would be a chore in tennis shoes. He hopped over a puddle and right into more mud, slick gray mud.

Mel tracked it to the front door and went inside, there was no mat to wipe them on inside or out then he managed to make it to the couch and removed them. Walking to the kitchen Mel stepped in some cat crap that Killer had left for Mel to find.

"Killer, you moron, why did you do that what's wrong with you, are you a nincompoop?" "Meow." "That's not good enough." "I will have to put you out in the cold wet rain!"

And it came to pass that Killer was put into the rain and wind then found refuge under the front porch. Meanwhile with killer in exile and a house that smelled foul Melvin worked on the problem of Max. He was the problem, he ruined everything, just like Killer! Aw but killer even with his faults was Melvin's friend and in a sorta simple way he was feeling remorseful for making his eyes cross. Yeah, that was a mean thing and he knew poor Killer had a rough time hunting. He thought it must be strange to be seeing double but catching nothing at all, poor Killer.

 Now back to the thought at hand what to do about max, that idiot. He didn't need to kill him no nothing like he used to do with small mice's at home, no this would just be disabling him. Like he had thought before, namely ruin his legs a little. This would take a lot of effort on Mel's part but he must begin. He found his favorite spot and he concentrated like never before and finally a bright white sphere appeared and Melvin held it in his hand and put all his hate and evil ambitions in it and let it fly away and out of site, would it work? He didn't know because it was such a task and such a distance then on the other hand he had such love and respect for Nancy the girl who gave him pickles and apples.

Mel let Killer back in, he was wet and cold and the two of them went to bed in the smelly house.

The traffic was light today and Melvin hurried to work and kept his ears open to see if any of what he did had come to fruition. "Good morning Nancy." "What's good about it?" "I don't know." "Oh, Melvin my boyfriend hurt himself last night." "What happened?" "Well they were going to load a truck up and he was standing in back of the truck and they didn't see him and they smashed his legs real bad the doctor says he might not walk again, isn't that awful?" "Um, sure I guess." "I better get to work." "You can say that again Melvin." "Oh, hi Wally glad to see your back." "I'll bet you slacker."

Mel kept his nose to the grindstone all day and thought to himself that he had accomplished his task. Lunch was around the corner and Nancy would be sitting with him again.

"Gee, I feel bad about your boyfriend, Nancy." "Yeah, it was the dumbest thing, he said the driver just wasn't watching then back into him with the big truck." "Oh well guess you'll have to get a new boyfriend." "You're crazy as hell, I'm going to marry that man." "Um, alright but if you need a new one." "You?" "Yes." "That would be a laugh, you'd be the last one, haw, ha."

Now That Hurt!

Mel's face turned red. He went back to work and thought to himself that she was a bad woman, she did not deserve him. He worked very hard. Mel kept his head down how could she the woman of his dreams. Now that was a joke, she was just like the others that treated Mel bad. Real mean like with little regard for his feelings. What kinda woman would give you a pickle and laugh at you like you were a joke just because you were just a little

Different than others, so unfair, he wanted to hurt her but couldn't bring himself to do it. And after all he had been up half the night crippling her boyfriend.

If only he hadn't maybe things would be back where they were yesterday. Mel had shot himself in the foot and couldn't tell a soul, except maybe Killer the cross eyed cat.

Sometimes love shows it's self in terms of sacrifice, it would have to be that way with Mel.

He would have to endure her to be around her, he would have to take her laughing at him to share lunch with her.

"Mel are you coming to eat lunch with me?" "Sure I guess." "Gee, sorry about your friend Nancy." "Oh Max, he's very strong and I'm sure we will get through this, I sure hope he don't lose his legs." "Can I have your pickle?" "Yes, Mel you rascal and my apple too, there are we friends again?" "Yes, thank you Nancy." "I didn't mean to laugh at you. I was just upset about Max, can you forgive me?" "Okay Nancy I love you." "Oh, Mel I love you too."

Then Nancy rubbed his head with her knuckle's as if to say (that's for luck). She went into the rest room for the remainder of the lunch break.

Mel tried to whistle at his sink, he was very happy.

"What the hell you so happy about you Moron, you aren't smart enough to know a fart from a sneeze." Wally continued. "Boy I sure didn't miss your sorry ass while I was laid up, now get with it halfwit!" "Sure Wally."

This was a roller coaster day and Wally had the down car. He hated Wally more and more, even Martha was better than this tyrant.

Well his adrenal gland was working overtime and Mel stared at the wall ahead of the sink, this day Wally get it again. He crossed Killers eyes, now his sites were on Wally, he would stare at that spot on the wall until Wally the rat was crossed eyed as well!

"Help I can't see, Nancy get out here I've fallen down and I can't get up?" "Eh, what's wrong Wally are you alright should I call the medics?" "Yes, call someone I can't see, everything's double I must be having another stroke."

Wally looked up at Nancy and he was as cross eyed as anyone she had ever seen.

"I'll call the medics right away Wally. Can I get a picture in case I don't ever see you again?" "Did you call?" "Oh yes, there on their way." "Say cheese!"

Nancy snapped a photo that would make a man on death row smile. Meanwhile the medic's loaded up Wally and took him to the clinic down the road. The whole restaurant grinded to a halt and everyone came out to watch Wally be taken away.

"Bye, bye Wally." "Yeah, good reddens to bad rubbish!" "Say, Nancy where are you hanging that photo when you print it out?" "Gee, I don't know maybe in the lunch room under the calendar so we could look when we want a good laugh, ha, haw." "Okay we will be checking daily."

 "Should we keep working?" "Yes, of course but take it easy for a change while the Ogre's away the subjects will play, ha haw." "Yeah, don't worry about us we will, ha haw."

The rest of the day moved swiftly. Then it was quitting time and Melvin ask Nancy if maybe he could take her down to dairy Queen for a Sunday, but for some strange reason she couldn't, being that she promised Max she would check on him after work. And the strangest thing was the more he looked at her the more cross eyed she was starting to look, probably in his head he guessed.

Mel was of course disappointed but could forgive her because he still wanted her company at some time in the future. Mel was very infatuated with her but things were moving slow if at all plus his stomach hurt just like his heart.

His love for her was so deep yet she was in a place that would never let him in and no matter how much he tried to make her love him, progress was so slow just like paint drying on an outhouse wall. Yes, Mel was aware that he was slower than most and well maybe even retarded to some degree. His mother called him special but deep down he knew that he was different. He remember the slurs of the kids in school and how their bullying had keep him back from reaching his full potential. The real problem wasn't that Mel didn't like himself but that others viewed him as inferior and that hurt in fact it hurt real bad.

Mel was very lucky though because he had a good job and was paying his own way now, if it wasn't for Wally it would be a perfect job. Mel had learned early own that like it or not there was a pecking order, he just happened to be at the bottom.

He went to the same grocery store he always went to and got a cart they were small but so were Mel's needs. He bought a jar of pickles some apples and a box of candy for Nancy he even thought of her while he shopped.

He needed sandwich bags and toilet paper. "Hi Melvin sorry about your folks it must be tough." "Ah, that's okay they were old I guess." "That they were Melvin, nineteen dollars and eighty three penny's my good man." "Here." Mel handed a crisp twenty dollar bill. "Here's your change seventeen cents, there you go buddy." "Thank you Mr. Spencer." "Say Melvin if you ever want to sell that truck, I'll buy it from you." "No, it was my dad's!" "Take it easy, just asking."

Mel left and burnt some rubber on the payment upon leaving, he was mad at old Spencer for asking about that truck, it was all he had to remember his father. He went straight home again. "HI, there Melvin my boy, just wanted to tell you I got some cows in the back yard but they shouldn't bother you much." "Anyway gota run."

Mel looked out his window in the back yard, there were ten of the biggest white face cows you had ever seen. They were all mooing and at different times, Mel hated them all. He had no idea what could be done and once again he sat and thought real hard about it. He couldn't kill all of them.

 They were much too large and if he hurt them they would cry all the more. He study them and noticed that when they mooed they put their heads up, so if he could keep their heads down just maybe they would be quite. That's it, he would make the muscle that holds their head up so weak that they would always be dragging the ground because that's where the grass is anyway.

And so it came to pass that all the cows in Mel's neighborhood developed weak neck muscles and their heads drooped to the ground. "Come on killer lets go to sleep and those pesky cows won't be noisy anymore." Killer agreed for he knew what happens to animals that defy Mel's wrath.

Morning came and so did the weekend. Mel gazed out his back window on the couch side of the house and just like he remember all the cows were grazing or dragging their head through the cow crap they left behind. In short it was an odd site with little noise just slow pathetic cows. Mel was pleased with himself although he did wonder how they would drink from the water trough.

Today was his day and he could do as he pleased sadly nothing interested him. Mel had no radio or television only his cross eyed cat. A man should have someone or something in his life.

After all isn't that what make life worth living? Poor Melvin slow to anger and slow to think how depressed he had become. He sat for a long time and done exactly nothing, he didn't even stare at the wall. With no purpose why bother who would care either way. Mel knew he had some problems but always was told not to worry he would out grow them. After some time Melvin decided to take a ride and some money and see if he could buy some entertainment of any kind. He went to the store downtown where his mother had always shopped. Lord how he missed her soft hands and gentle voice. She always had words of encouragement while his dad only criticisms. Yes, his father would say thinks like I hope you fail or I told you so and you'll never be as great as me, you are a fool.

"Can I help you?" "Um, my mom used to shop here." "That's nice, maybe a new oven?" "No." "Refrigerator maybe?" "No." "Okay I give up what do you want." "Um something I can do at home." "Like what?" "Do you have a television?" "Boy, did you come to the right store." "I have hundreds of them, so what's it going to be large or small?" "Smaller than a window." "Gee thanks for the clue." "Maybe about the size of a small chair." "Oh brother got a live one here, follow me and don't trip on anything." "Um, okay I won't." "Look at these and decide I'll be back in a while." "I need a break."

Mel looked and also checked the prices, they were very expensive and he would have to get a very small one. Mel waited for the salesman to return for over an hour then as if a miracle had happened he did.

"Ah, ha good choice and if you didn't know it is a radio as well, good choice son good choice." "Now follow me up to the counter and we will relieve you of your money, ha haw." "Yes." "Will there be anything else?" "Yes, I want my mom back." "Can't help you their buddy well, you have a nice day." "Okay I will."

Mel hurried home and put his combo on the bookshelf in the front room of the house. He plugged in the cord and turned it on. Mel fooled with it for some time but could never receive a picture. Then he discovered a button mark audio receiver and turned that on and behold music. So many stations he had a world of music and info at his command he would overlook the bad reception of the television. He found a station with some piano music and listen to it, which was as pure as anything he could ever comprehend. It made this weekend a joy to be home alone. The music to Mel was companion to his depression plus made him wish Nancy was by his side. If only she could feel his pain maybe she would understand.

 Women what do they know about love. Mel's dad had once said they only care for themselves. He used to also say they only have the morals that men give them because they can't fully understand matters of the heart. He never thought about what his dad had ever said before but it was like he could now hear his words. If only Nancy could feel his pain. He would make her know it was the only way.

This time listening to some soft soothing music he channeled all his thought in to one central point it was much more defined than ever before, so pure and bright as love its self and then Melvin poured all his pain for love into it. He put in the hopelessness the emptiness from when they were apart and even the hungry feeling in his stomach, just like the feeling he felt when both of his folks died and the day he had to move out. It was all so sad and in a strange way pure and beautiful.

He projected the type of love that makes people kill themselves. The shear emptiness and desperation of a man in a shallow well yelling for help and hearing voices but no one come to the edge and even looks over. When all of it was wrapped in his ultra-white sphere he sent it in Nancy's direction.

The rest of the weekend Mel just laid on the couch petting Killer the cross eyed cat and listening to his new friend namely the radio.

Mondays come quickly and the weekends leave us so much quicker. Mel was driving in to work one more time. His dads old Chevrolet pickup run good and he racked the pipes some because he liked the hot rod sound. He whipped it into the parking lot and sprayed a little gravel towards

Wally's new car. "Mel you idiot where did you get you license?" "I know in a crackerjack box huh?" "Don't know." "You wouldn't next time you come in slowly and don't even get a speck of gravel on my car." "Okay Wally." "Sheeze, grow a brain will you!" "Alright." "Hello Nancy, I missed you." "And I missed you to Mel strangely like never before are you okay I heard Wally picking on you?" "Yes, I'm okay." "Still want to have lunch with me?" "Why yes, I wouldn't miss it for the world." "Oh boy see you then." "Mel, did I ever tell you that your cute?" "No." "Well, you are."

Nancy walked by and brushed him as if to say I am yours. Mel worked tirelessly today in great anticipation for lunch plus every now and then Nancy would walk by and smile at him.

"Hey Mel what did you do to make Nancy like you?" "Oh, I don't Know Bert she just does I guess." "Well I'll be a monkeys Uncle!" "I have been here as long as or longer than you and she never gave me the time of day." "Hell, you wouldn't know what to do if you caught her, maybe that what she likes about you she feels safe yeah, that's gota be it I guess." "Guess so."

Mel went to lunch and Nancy set next to Mel and shared her lunch with him and spoke in a baby language that maybe only the two of them connected on. So pure and innocent and yet creepy all the same.

Mel, I missed you something awful." "Yes and so did I." "Do you want to be my girlfriend?" "Oh, yes Mel, yes I do." "I guess I should tell Max though." "I hope he won't be mad." "Mad, he will go bonkers you will have to leave or I am as sure as I am setting here he won't stop till you are dead." I"I better go back to work now can I have that last cookie?" "Haven's yes, take it."

Back at work with a cross eyed boss and a cat to match at home, Mel thought about what sweet Nancy had warned him about, he knew that his legs were smashed but of course they would mend and he would come for Mel to ruin his one shot at haven. This weighed heavy on Mel's mind he had never killed anything before and he remember from Sunday school that he wasn't supposed to do it.

Then on some level it occurred to Melvin that he need not kill anything just keep it at bay by making Max a cripple. Mel knew it was better than killing and who's to say, maybe he just got worse and that's all. Melvin stared and worked then when he was washing the plates he felt that bright orb that always brung him relief and he made his will, its will. The bright sphere just like Elvis left the building.

"Why are you crying Nancy?" "Oh, Mel it's so terrible Max is going to lose his legs and never be able to walk again." "Gee, I don't want to see you cry Nancy can I do anything?" "You?" "Melvin your hearts in the right place but this one is beyond us, it's up to God now." "Um, okay I guess." "Can I take you to Dairy Queen for a Sunday?" "Sure, why not."

Mel cranked his Chev hard and into the driveway of the Dairy Queen restaurant. Mel got out of his truck and walked to the other side and let Nancy out.

"Boy, I could get used to this." "Max never would do anything nice like that for me." "Really, why not?" "Oh, I was just his eye candy and he knew if any one looked at me he would smash them like a bug, ya see I lived in fear of whoever would challenge him." "You mean like me?" "You?"

"He always thought you were retarded and I would never have anything at all to do with you." "Was he right?" "Well up till this morning I'd have to say yes, but now you seem so much more than what you are." "Um, oh." "What you two want?" "Two Sunday's strawberry large please." "Sure coming up." "How did you know what kind I liked?" "I just do." "You are a strange one what else do I need to know about you?" "I got wax in my ear." "Nope, that wasn't it." "I got a cat." "Yeah, you said that." "Is he a good mouser?" "No, I think it's his eyes their not for hunting." "You crack me up, is this the one you said was cross eyed?" "Yes." "Gee, how did he get that way?"

"I done it he was bad." "Alright if that's what you think, but how?" "With my brain." "Ha haw, haw that's funny, stop it you're killing me ha haw!" "I like you, you laugh that's good." "Yes, Mel that's very good." "Well Mel take me to my car and I'll see you at work tomorrow alright sweetie?" "Okay, I guess."

They put their dirty wrappers away and Mel drove her to her car. Nancy kissed Mel on the cheek like his mother used to do. It was enough. Mel drove home with a smile and a feeling of love he had never ever know before.

Every good day has its counterparts, that is to say you can't have a good without a bad. This day was just like that because when Mel reached home he learned his neighbor's to the right and in between him and the all too nosy landlord had just got a pair of loud dogs that bark continually. He knew they were vicious and other than yell he had nothing at all to do with them.

"You dogs be quite, do you hear me stop that barking stop that barking or you're going to get it."

They barked on louder and very excessively. Mel went inside and full of rage for dogs that would pay him no mind he sat down where he could work on his problem. He thought about their voice box and how that might affect their eating and ruled that out. Something had to work if only he could be smart enough to figure it out. Then like a rocket out of the future it came to him. He would make their tongues ten inches longer then they would be so busy tasting things that they would forget to bark. What on heavens earth could be wrong with a plan like this?

And so in the days of Mel it came to pass that these things took place and Mel step out on to the porch to behold his miracle and lay his eyes on how in Mel's world he had improved on the God's design.

"It worked, just as I thought it would." They have all stopped barking and as planned they were busy dragging their tongues through the dirt. Then behold another side effect miracle they now were ever so careful where they crapped. Felling full of himself and suddenly very tired Mel and Killer lay down and went to sleep.

Early to bed and early to rise helps make a man healthy, wealthy and wise or at least that's what his mother used to always say. Mel was up at the crack of dawn and after saying good bye to Killer went out to his truck he stared over where the dogs were and they saw him and stopped wagging their tails as if to say you're the one that did this to us. Their tongues were out about a foot and dragging on the ground, truly a very unusual site. Mel shrugged it off and climbed into the truck.

Now most people would have some remorse of their actions but most people were not Melvin, he was special.

"Good Morning Nancy." "Well, hello stranger and a good morning to you as well Melvin." "Just Mel please." "Okay, I just like Melvin sometimes." "That's okay, this time." "You say the funniest things, I'll see you at lunch." "Yes you will."

If Melvin could have he would have whistled he was very content with his station in life and with his own place plus a cat plus Nancy to love whatever could go wrong. Mel worked faster and accidentally dropped a plate.

"Ka-smash!" "What the hell is going on back there?" "Melvin is that you?" "Are you okay?" "Yes, I broke a plate." "Might know it would be you." "You clumsy fool, don't you have any damned brains at all?" "Yes." "Well listen Einstein you clean this mess up before that pea brain of yours shorts out completely!" "Yes." "Your pathetic you lousy poor excuse for a human being. It is a wonder you can put your pants on!" "Now get your ass to work, for a change!"

This hurt Mel's feeling real bad but he had taken Wally's abuse so long he wasn't sure how to act, he just kept it inside. Nancy sensed it bothered him greatly and she scolded Wally for being mean to him.

"Wally that wasn't nice you know he's got issues why do you belittle him so?" "Cause he's a turd and turds are a dime a dozen!" "Kinda like you waitresses so just keep talking lady and you will find yourself on the other side of that front door!" "You wouldn't dare!" "Don't test me now I suggest you get back up on that front counter and keep your nose out of other people's business!" "Sure Wally, sure!" "Hope you don't come up short." "What's that supposed to mean?" "Nothing I'm working now so can you leave me alone?" "Yes, I will but if I'm one nickel short your history!"

After sticking her tongue out at Wally behind his back Nancy buried herself in her work until Lunch.

"Hey, Nancy you shouldn't make Wally mad he could fire you." "Oh, I know he just makes me so mad and with those cross eyes he's easy to pick on." "Sorta like me huh?" "Oh, Mel what's wrong with you aint your fault but Wally is rotten to the core." "Thank you Nancy." "That man hurt my feelings." "I know Mel, I know."

When Mel finished cleaning his ear with his finger and looking at it, he said, "Can I have your Twinkie Nancy?" "Oh Mel, if only you could truly understand what happens in this Loony bin." "Aw, but it's a living I guess and a job is a job." "Uh huh, did you bring a pickle?" "No, Mel I am all out at home, no pickle." "We could get some after work?" "No, Mel I'm starting to think you and I are getting just a little too close." "You see I was taking advantage of you and that's unfair. It's just so hard." "I know." "Ah, Mel I got to recount the money for Wally again."

Nancy went back up front and left a half of a boloney sandwich and Mel supposed she left it for him and he ate it.

Back in the kitchen it was still, steamy and sullen. Mel thought about what had happened to day but one thing for sure Nancy affection for him was taking a freight train out of town hell bent for Chicago. He was a lot more careful with the dishes though.

Time to go home and maybe get Nancy back in his good spot he never hug her but imagine her to be nice and soft just like his old teddy bear. Yes, the one his father threw in the fireplace on Christmas Eve five years ago.

"Nancy you want to go to Dairy Queen again, for ice cream? "Nope, going to see Max tonight they say the news is better." "But, how could it be?" "I have been praying Mel and sometimes he hears us." "You mean God?" "Yes, now I have to go so let go of me and let me by." Nancy looked into Melvin's eyes as if to say please. "Okay, see you tomorrow alligator." "That's see you later alligator." "Okay crocodile." "Gota go."

Mel watched her drive out of site, a tear rolled down his cheek he knew even with all his ways she would never be with him because he was special. Mel drove slowly home to his friend the cat.

 After listening to Elvis a while on the radio Mel was thinking very romantic thoughts about him and Nancy. The girl he was just too special to get. It seemed if everything he had changed didn't help him win her maybe he would have to do what a lot of lost lovers have done in the past he would have to change himself into a real person. Someone like the produce salesman that wore suits and talked sharply. Someone who wasn't so special. If only he could. Mel had never tried to change himself. He had always try to bend things to teach them a lesson and make them behave how he wanted them to act.

 He would have to try but if he was able how would he know? Maybe he could smear peanut butter on the mirror yes big letters that said just, "Special." That might just do it. Then with Killer he sat down on the couch and he began to imagine how it would be and how smart he would become. He saw his self for the first time standing up for himself to Wally and having lunch with Bert and the other workers at the restaurant. And of course the main prize being able to hold unto the thought of loving someone with his whole heart even more than a pickle, he would have to try. Melvin wanted this more than anything anyone had ever wanted in their life. He stared deeply and slipped into a trance and as he did white snowballs of bright light slowly surrounded him. The sprinkles of light fell upon his nose like a sparkler of thought and when the room was full they had consumed him.

Mel awoke and stretched. It was a day like many other days somewhat overcast and according to the news a slight chance of rain. Mel fooled with the television and discovered there was no antenna lead in wire he would have to buy one.

 He shaved, brushed his teeth and cleaned all the piles of cat crap from the floor, mental note to self also buy litter box for killer. Melvin read the box as he ate his cereal and he washed the bowl and cleaned the table then counter. The spoon was wash off and put in with the knife and fork in the drawer. Mel grabbed his newly made lunch then locked the door of his house and walked to his truck, he wished the dogs would stop barking, but dogs will be dogs he guess and started his truck.

Twenty miles later and ten minutes early he arrived at work.

"Good morning Nancy you look nice today, new dress?" "Why yes, and thank you Mel!" "Guess I better get to it."

Wally seen Nancy and Mel talking and decided to warn Mel about it one more time.

"Well, Mell you moron you like working here?" "Not much Wally, kissing your fat ass aint my idea of fun why?" "You idiot you can't talk to me that way." "Why not you cross eye tub of lard, why not?" "Because after I slug you I'll fire you that's why!" "Go ahead Wally I'd love to get the cops in here maybe after I call the health department to complain about the damned rats I will!" "You wouldn't dare!" "Watch me you nincompoop!" "Hey, that's what I call you, you can't call me that!" "Just did, why you got another dishwasher for today, I hear this is a very busy day with a lot of rich folks leaving big tips coming in. Think you want to risk it?" "No I guess not." "Well, Wally the walrus, I don't know how you're going to get by without a dish washer tomorrow but I guess you're going to find out because at the end of my shift I get my check and all you will see is my taillights, happy now?" "Maybe, but quit talking to Nancy will you?" "About that, I have your home number and Martha probably would like to know what her fat crossed eyed husband is so worried about with the pretty help." "You wouldn't?" "Now are you going to start being nice to me and Nancy, or should I make things bad for you, you weasel?" "Oh, alright, Good morning to you too!"

Melvin said not another word but went straight to work and put in a good days work till noon.

"Nancy how was max?" "Oh he's doing better but it will be a while before he can get full use of his legs again. " "Thanks for asking Melvin you're turning into a fine young man, one might say even a gentleman." "Thanks, Nancy that's the nicest thing you ever said to me." "Well, I heard how you stuck up for yourself with Wally, and believe you me everybody here felt just like you." "Good for you Mel."

Then she planted a big kiss right on his cheek.

"Would you like to have my pickle, I bought some more?" "No, I don't care for them anymore, I guess I out grew them." "I am so impressed, Mel, your like talking to a new you." "Thanks again pretty woman." "What are you going to do when you leave tomorrow?" "Oh, I don't know I heard my father left me a whole bunch of money thought maybe if I could find some nice gal to go with me I might just travel and look at stuff, then come back and go to veterinary school, I always did like animals." "Why did I know that about you?" "Wow, you know we got a lot in common and I was thinking of quitting, could I be that gal?" "Oh, I don't know think I'll look around a little, beside what about Max?" "Max who?"

Melvin just cracked the biggest grin of his lifetime, funny how were not always as we let people see us but more like how we imagine are very best selves to be.

"Let me call my mother so she can break it to him that I left." "From now on I'm traveling with you!" "Think it's that easy?" "Isn't it?" "Well, I hear we got to get some passports first." "Oh, yeah sure that's just what I was thinking."

"You too going to quit without any notice?" "Wally, you should get them eyes fixed before you have another stroke or something were leaving out of this crappy place and we aint coming back!" "Well, don't expect me to give you two any good reference!" "Don't worry this would be the last place we would ever use!"

Melvin and Nancy got in Mel's truck and drove away.

Mel and Nancy did get their passports and hopped on a cruise ship to the Caribbean. Rumor has it their making wedding plans.

And the reports of bright white orbs of light in the sky were pass off as either U. F O.'s or weather balloons.

Mel's power of telekinesis never returned to him and yes some animals for some reason stay as he left them. As for those that were affected by his extraordinary pettiness, well shall we say that they are under very good hands of some very special physician?

 Oh, about the cat, Killer? As hard as it is to believe when Mel returned home that last evening and cleaned the peanut butter from the mirror he remember what he done. He took killer with him to his new home. While the dogs fully recovered the horses never did and are living their Live's out on a ranch for abused animals in Washington State.

The End

About The Author

Irvin Johnson

Resides in the Evergreen State of Washington.

He lives in the Capitol city.

Puts on car show in the third weekend of June at O'Blarneys Irish Pub and Restaurant.

Enjoys a morning cup of coffee with friends

Has five other novels to his credit

Old 99, 2008

Flight 3, 2016

Maggie, 2017

Delwin, Betty and boomer, 2016

Where's Fred? 2017

Dedication

This book is dedicated to those in search of their better selves.

This is to urge them that toil tirelessly day after day for someone else, that help is just around the corner.

Now is the time to reach inside ourselves and do something to make each day a little better than the day before.

IRV

Printed in Great Britain
by Amazon